ONE DIRECTION

CONFIDENTIAL

UNAUTHORIZED

BARRON'S

All inquiries should be addressed to:
Barron's Educational Series, Inc.
250 Wireless Boulevard,
Hauppauge, New York 11788
www.barronseduc.com

ISBN: 978-1-4380-0502-7

Library of Congress Control Number: 2013955115

Date of Manufacture: December 2013
Manufactured by: Oriental Press, Dubai, UAE

Printed in Dubai, UAE

9 8 7 6 5 4 3 2 1

PLEASE NOTE: This book is not affiliated with or endorsed
by One Direction or any of their publishers or licensees.

CONTENTS

1D RULE THE WORLD

One Direction is the world's biggest and most beloved boy band. Of that there can be no doubt. From their very first appearance as five boys united under one name, on the U.K.'s *X Factor* in 2010, these very talented and lucky boys from Britain have gone on to sell out stadium shows at home and abroad in seconds; become three-dimensional film stars in their own movie, *This Is Us* (which went on to become the biggest grossing documentary of 2013); prolifically release chart-topping singles and record-breaking albums—not to mention clock-up billions of YouTube views for their award-winning music videos.

Their achievements do not stop there. With their loyal, loud, and super-screaming fans—known as Directioners—One Direction have also pioneered new changes in communicating with their audience (via their Vine videos, YouTube channel, and Twitter accounts) allowing them to have more direct contact with the fans who mean so much to them, and to say thank you for their love and endless support. To the band, it's the fans that always come first.

But more important than all their success and fame, One Direction are without a doubt five of the nicest and most genuine boys and international pop stars you could ever hope to meet.

Zayn, Liam, Niall, Louis, and Harry—they, and they alone, forever will be, One Direction. None of them could be replaced without severely upsetting the unique chemistry these five boys have formed. They are the best of friends, brothers, each one of them united by the desire to produce the best music they can while having as much fun as they can squeeze out of the experience as possible.

One Direction Confidential is your one-stop shop to the world's greatest boy band of all time, your access-all-areas VIP pass to the boys up close and personal, and as you've always wanted to see them —100 percent real—and yours to forever hold in your hands!

1D IN NORTH AMERICA

North America has some of the world's best One Direction fans, and the boys have enjoyed mega-success on U.S. soil—a dream they never thought would ever come true.

▶ Live and loud at Verizon Center, Washington D.C., June 23, 2013.

With the instant success of *Up All Night* —the album went straight to number one in the U.S. and Canada—selling over a million records in the first week, the band became the first British group in U.S. chart history to achieve this feat with a debut album. How's that for an impressive start? The band's second album, *Take Me Home,* also broke records and ended up, alongside *Up All Night*, in the U.S.'s top five best selling albums of the same 12-month period! A massive achievement, not only for a British group, but also for a band that was only one year old!

The band also became the first U.K. group to have their debut album enter the U.S. chart at number one. Now, with *Midnight Memories* in 2013, all three of the quintet's albums have entered into the U.S. top five! America has been well and truly broken by One Direction!

Awards, records, and private jets to their own gigs might be nice accessories to have, but at the end of the day, the band's most treasured moments are performing every night to their loyal fans who buy tickets, line up outside the venue, and take time off school (or have to plead their parents to let them go). And on the U.S., Canadian, and Mexican leg of their *Up All Night* and *Take Me Home Tours*, there were definitely *a lot* of fans!

Performing 22 songs each gig, at the end of the show the band is exhausted! In fact, they were so exhausted at the end of the North American leg of the *Take Me Home Tour* that Harry was left emotional and unable to thank the fans without getting a tear in his eye. "That's it. North American tour over, and I have been left speechless

▲ Niall waves hello to 20,000 fans at the AmericanAirlines Arena, Miami, June 14, 2013.

"SELLING OUT MADISON SQUARE GARDEN WAS PRETTY AMAZING. THEN WE WOKE TO THE NEWS THAT OUR U.K. TOUR WAS SOLD OUT. IT WAS CRAZY!"
HARRY

▲ Niall makes working hard look good onstage, wearing his beloved Little White Lies T-shirt.

"WHEN WE GOT PUT TOGETHER AS
A GROUP, WE COULDN'T IMAGINE
OURSELVES COMING TO AMERICA,
LET ALONE RELEASING OUR ALBUM
HERE, SO FOR US TO BE SITTING AT
THE TOP OF THE U.S. ALBUM CHARTS
IS UNBELIEVABLE."
LIAM

▲ The boys show off their glorious suntans after a long day filming the music video for "Best Song Ever," Miami, Florida, June 13, 2013.

▼ Perfoming "Best Song Ever" on the *Today Show*, New York, the band brought the city that never sleeps to a standstill, August 23, 2013.

▲ Louis and Harry share a joke onstage, Target Center, Minneapolis, June 18, 2013.

▲ Thousands of Directioners lined the New York city streets as the band performed "Little Things" on the *Today Show*, August 23, 2013.

◀ Directioners as far as the eye can see, the *Today Show*, New York, August 23, 2013.

by your continued support. Without you, we don't exist ... so thank you."

But their U.S. tour in 2013 didn't all smell of sweet success. At a gig at the First Midwest Bank Amphitheater, Chicago (during the beginning of the U.S. leg of the *Take Me Home Tour*), Harry's famously curly hair was set on fire! During the end of their cover of "Teenage Dirtbag" Harry walked to the side of the stage to wipe his brow with a towel. While the towel was on his head, Harry was unaware that it had been set on fire by one of the lights above him! Thankfully, the quick-thinking actions of brave bandmate Zayn, who noticed that Harry was heading straight into the flames, quickly pulled him out of danger. The towel was set alight, but thankfully Harry's hair wasn't too singed —talk about a close shave!

▲ Team 1D: Wearing the Division C jersey of the Montreal Canadiens, the band plays Montreal's Bell Center, July 4, 2013.

Harry's bad luck doesn't end there. While performing in Pittsburgh, Pennsylvania, also on the *Take Me Home Tour*—as well as once in Melbourne, Australia—poor Harry had to run off stage to be sick several times. Thankfully, it wasn't because he was ill—it was because he had eaten too much before the show; "I think everyone thinks it's because I was drinking," he said afterward, "but it was actually because I had dinner too close to stage time and I was just so full!" Hopefully, Harry will have more luck on the U.S. leg of the *Where We Are Tour* in summer 2014!

PROFILE:
NIALL

The Nialler may look like the most innocent of the group, but as the fourth youngest in the band, it's his duty to forever smile and strum his way out of all the trouble he causes!

Regarded as one of the funniest members of the band—before Harry came up with the name One Direction, Niall suggested the band should be called "Niall and the Potatoes!"—Niall is also one of the most poignant and passionate about the band's personal achievements, beautiful fans, and triumphant online and worldwide success.

Born in Ireland on September 13 1993, the only non-English member of the band carries with him everywhere he goes his strong Irish heritage and a deep sense of where he came from (not to mention his cute accent). "I used to get kicked out of class for singing Irish traditional songs," Niall once explained, unable to hide his beaming Irish pride and desire to perform.

Niall has over 15 million followers on Twitter (and counting!) and is very proactive on the site, constantly letting his fans know his plans, leading the band to constantly play-fight over who has gained the biggest number of followers!

◀ Moments before a show in Sydney, Australia, Niall kicks back and relaxes backstage, October 5, 2013.

▶ A winning smile: Niall at the 2013 MTV Video Music Awards where 1D won Song of the Summer, August 26, 201

▲ The Nialler takes center stage at Brisbane's Convention and Exhibition Center, Australia, April 18, 2012.

▲ Looking classy at the JLS Foundation and Cancer Research U.K. fundraiser, London, England, June 6, 2013.

◄ Niall showing off his most-recent MTV Moonman win on the *Today Show*, New York, August 23, 2013.

NIALL

Birthplace: Mullingar, County Westmeath, Ireland

Zodiac sign: Virgo

Favorite musicians: Oasis, Coldplay, The Eagles, Bon Jovi, Michael Bublé

Favorite color: Green

Hobbies: Eating!

As one of the most romantic, and single, members of the band—as well the most elusive when it comes to girls—Niall forever wears his heart on his sleeve, and can often be caught talking in interviews about how much he can't wait to fall in love. "I can't wait for the day I marry a Directioner," he has teased his fans recently.

As the only member of the band who frequently performs on stage with an electric and acoustic guitar, many fans have picked up that while he may be left-handed, he plays the guitar with his right hand, which is impressive. He also let it slip that he's been dying his hair since he was 12, but keep that secret to yourself!

Following the release of their number one album, *Midnight Memories* in 2013, and

their first stadium world tour, Niall is also the subject of affection of many of the band's female fans—not to mention a few female celebrity admirers as well. Both Demi Lovato and Katy Perry have admitted to admiring Niall, forcing him to admit he gets a bit light-headed every time he sees the "Fireworks" singer. "Katy Perry gets me every time. She's very funny in person. We met at the Teen Choice Awards and she told me how cute I was. My life was literally flashing before my eyes," he said.

Though a confident and excitable performer onstage, Niall has confessed that he still gets nervous before each live show. "When we first started out, the thought of getting up on stage freaked us all out," he remembers. "The kind of crowds we get are very, very loud, which helps actually. The bigger the crowd, the better really! The noise calms your nerves."

▲ Enjoying some soccer at Newcastle United FC training ground, Newcastle, England, April 10, 2013.

▶ At the season finale of *The X Factor*, Los Angeles, California, December 20, 2012.

"OUR BAND WILL NEVER CHANGE, WE WILL ALWAYS BE FIVE SINGING IDIOTS."
NIALL

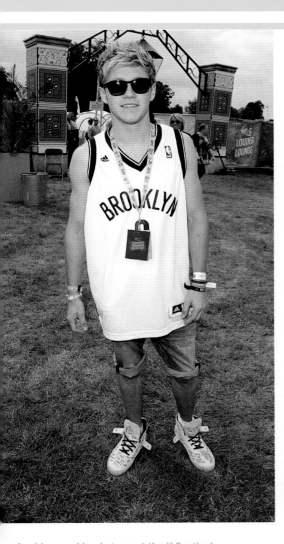

▲ Looking cool backstage at the V Festival, Chelmsford, England, August 17, 2013.

◀ Sitting as he strums a C chord, Niall performs in New York, August 23, 2013.

Though playing guitar on the recording of *Midnight Memories* made Niall very happy, his personal highlight of the band's success so far was undeniably when "*Up All Night* went to No.1 in America!" he remarked. "The top four that week was us, Adele, Guns N' Roses, and Bruce Springsteen. It was ridiculous seeing us amongst those names!" The album went on to sell over four million copies in the U.S.!

During *The X Factor U.K.* 2010, guest judge Katy Perry let Niall through to the next stages of the competition, on the proviso he was "not to let her down." The day the band's debut album came out in the U.S. (and went straight to Number One) Katy tweeted Niall, writing, "Congratulations, you didn't let me down." How sweet!

▲ Singing his heart out at the Vector Arena, Auckland, New Zealand, October 12, 2013.

▲ On a well deserved day off, the boys unwind on a speedboat in Sydney Harbor, Australia, April 10, 2012.

▶ Smell of success: Promoting their first fragrance, "Our Moment," in London, England, June 6, 2013.

FUN DIRECTION

Belonging to the world's biggest boy band may be a lot of hard work (it certainly looks like it!), but in between hectic tour schedules, and promotions, the guys like to have their own space to go a little crazy!

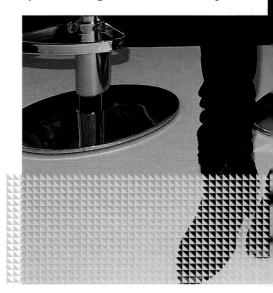

Whether it's soccer, surfing, boxing, hanging out with old friends or famous new ones, the boys have many hobbies and interests outside of the band to help them relax and unwind—golf appears to be the most recent band hobby they all enjoy! But no matter where they are, or whatever they are doing, they are never far from each other ... or their fans, staying in constant contact.

Since forming in 2010, the boys have worked nonstop, with very little time off. While the secret to their success is most definitely hard work, 100 percent commitment, catchy songs and a whole lot

▲ 1D playing with their official dolls in Westwood, California, August 6, 2013.

◀ Louis and Niall posing for the crowd, Vector Arena, Auckland, New Zealand, October 12, 2013.

of talent and luck, much of the band's charm and likeability comes from the fact that the 1D boys are best friends. It's obvious that the boys genuinely love one another, even if they sometimes get sick of spending so much time in each other's company ... not to mention Niall's farting.

When not on tour, making yet another music video, or attending a public appearance or award show (of which, these days, there have been plenty!) the band enjoys nothing more than taking time off for

some well deserved fun, or in Niall's case "not moving from the couch ... watching DVDs all day!", as he recently tweeted at the end of the earth-shattering *Take Me Home Tour*.

In between strict tour schedules, the band can be seen out and about all over the place. Each member has his own interests outside of the band: Harry his fashion and art, Louis loves soccer, Zayn loves to draw, Liam loves boxing, and Niall loves to eat! A few of the boys' also love to surf; they have been spotted breaking waves, with their newly

▲ Stars in stripes: Taking a break at the Newcastle FC training ground, Newcastle, England, April 10, 2013.

▼ Moments before performing "One Thing" at the MTV VMAs, Los Angeles, California, September 6, 2012.

acquired six packs, while on their recent gigs in Australia. They can often be seen around London too—their current base of operations—enjoying a variety of events, venues and, of course, the nightlife— forever followed and photographed for the next day's newspapers.

Each member also loves to spend time with his family. Their moms and dads and siblings are super-important to them, as seen so beautifully in their movie *This Is Us,* especially in that heartbreaking scene when Liam's mom cries because she misses her newly famous son so much!

▲ The band goes back to school: Backstage Creations Celebrity Retreat, Gibson Amphitheater, Universal City, California, August 11, 2013.

◀ Zayn takes aim at a Private Concert and Fan Chat, Westwood, California, August 6, 2013.

"I DO HAVE A LOT OF FUN, BUT I'M NOT HALF AS BUSY AS I'M MADE OUT TO BE, THAT'S FOR SURE."
HARRY

1D IN EUROPE

If you've been lucky enough to see the band over the past few years, you'll know just how exciting and thrilling one of their gigs can be. Their *Up All Night Tour*, their first ever, sold out all sixty shows in a matter of minutes—wow!

One Direction are amazing performers. And they absolutely love to play live. It's where, they have all said, their hearts belong the most. Being up close with the crowd, performing as best as they can, and generally goofing around with one another is what makes all the hard work and early mornings worthwhile. Yes, the boys may have over half a billion views on YouTube for their debut music video "What Makes You Beautiful," and, yes, their faces may appear on the bestselling U.K. calendar of all time, and, yes, they may well be the "new Take That" (according to their mentor, "Uncle" Simon Cowell), but beyond all their fame and successes, the band are at their happiest when they are performing live onstage to a sea of smiling and screaming fans. Having already performed on two sell-out tours around the world, the *Up All Night Tour* in 2011–12 and the *Take Me Home Tour* of 2013, the band are no strangers to shaking their stuff live onstage to tens of thousands of girls—and some boys too, of course. The band's lengthy and exhausting tours across Europe have rapidly grown in size, trying to squeeze in as many shows as they can to reach as many of their worldwide fans as possible.

On their first tour, the boys played to over 20 arenas across Europe, their second tour saw them play to over 60 arenas, and now on their most recent tour, the band will be seen playing to over 30 stadiums across Europe, including three sold-out shows at London's legendary Wembley Stadium, and three jam-packed shows in Ireland at Dublin's massive Croke Park—which will make Niall smile

▲ Five become One: The *Take Me Home Tour* played over 60 European dates, beginning at London's O2 Arena.

from ear-to-ear, for sure! Most of the tickets sold out within minutes for each of their new European shows, setting various records at many of the venues.

Usually bulging with the biggest hits from all their albums to date, as well as a medley of covers—from Natalie Imbruglia's "Torn" to Wheatus' "Teenage Dirtbag"—a One Direction show is full of lights, pyrotechnics, lasers, flames, dry ice, explosions, and super-massive video screens—perfect for seeing the band in high-definition, even if you're right at the back of the arena!

▲ Stopping off at Oberhausen, Berlin, Hamburg, and Munich, the boys delight their German fans.

"I HOPE THAT I'D STILL BE TOURING WITH ONE DIRECTION IN 10 YEARS' TIME. I LOVE THIS JOB SO MUCH—IF YOU NEED TO CALL IT A JOB."
HARRY

Having played hundreds of shows over such a short span of time has made the boys become incredibly gifted and thrilling performers.

It's no secret that the band tries to incorporate as few rehearsed dance moves into stage shows and their music videos as possible. They love to sing and jump around in their own style—but aren't so into the "cheesy dance moves" used by other boy bands. The band's choreographer, Paul Roberts, has told the fans that the boys hate to "synchronize their dance steps," preferring to be "more organic" when onstage. "They are naturally brilliant performers and they are very good at being aware of each other onstage, and unselfish," Paul says, "but when it comes to rehearsing dance moves, the boys just want to go onstage and have fun instead,"—and they most certainly do!

Touring all over Europe is very hard work, as any band or musician will agree. But thankfully, the band can lean on one another to help get them through long and grueling times away from home. Plus, the boys create havoc with

▲ Onstage in Autogrammstunde, Cologne, the boys are all smiles for the cameras, September 22, 2012.

◀ Floating high above their French fans, 1D wows the crowd, Paris, Galaxie Amnéville, April 29, 2013.

◀ Zayn's naughty streak: Sporting a funky blonde quiff, the Zaynster sings to his fans, November 2, 2012.

▲ Clowning around on Sweden's *The X Factor*, November 2, 2012.

their musicians too—that always helps to fight the tour bus blues! "One night, I think we were in Madrid—we taped up our band's door so they couldn't get out of the dressing room before the gig!" remembers Harry.

With the band having performed over 100 shows across Europe so far, and with many more scheduled for their *Where We Are Tour*, they know all the ingredients to putting on a great gig. Zayn has his top off, Niall breaks out his guitar, Liam's strong pop voice belts out an amazing solo, and Harry's jokes and flirty grin can be seen in super-fine detail on the massive TV screens.

The band, just before having a pre-show group hug—and leaping out energetically onto the stage—have a funny ritual of eating candy together. "We toast the sweets like they're drinks. We 'cheers' them," says Louis. "It's very strange, but it's for good luck!"

While on tour around Europe, the band performed many public appearances at local radio stations and TV stations. While recording their *Take Me Home* album in Stockholm (for six months) the band also appeared on the Swedish version of *The X Factor*. While most bands who appear on the show only get to perform one song, One Direction, being special of course, performed two—"What Makes You Beautiful" and "Live While We're Young," instantly rocketing them to No.1. Again.

PROFILE:
ZAYN

The second oldest in the band, Zayn Malik, is also the most brooding and intense, his eyes hinting at a maturity far beyond his years. Translated into English from Arabic, his name "Beautiful" (Zayn) "King" (Malik) is pretty accurate in our opinion!

Born on January 12, 1993, Zayn's road to mega-stardom with the band almost didn't happen. In 2009, the initially shy and very unconfident 17-year-old pulled out of *The X Factor* auditions due to nerves and stage fright. We don't blame him though —performing in front of the judges must be terrifying!

Zayn almost walked off the show during the Bootcamp stage when he felt he couldn't dance as well as the other boys. Thankfully, judge Simon Cowell stepped in and instilled some confidence in him. Zayn went on to wow the judges with his song choice, and his place in the band was assured—but it was a close call for a few minutes! Zayn also got the last laugh though, as now One Direction take pride in being members of the world's best boy band—who don't dance.

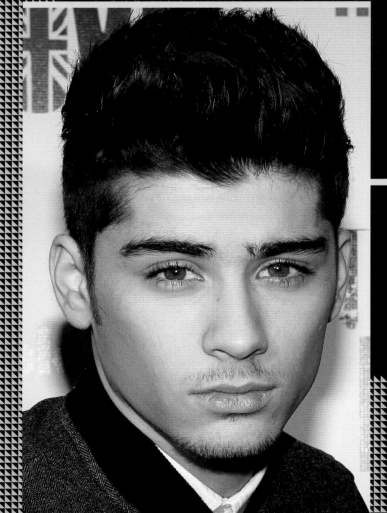

◀ Zayn looking hot, New York, March 8, 2012.

> " I LOVE THE FACT I GREW UP WANTING A BROTHER AND NOW I HAVE FOUR."
> ZAYN

▲ Singing from the heart: Zayn thanks the fans during the matinee performance, Hordern Pavilion, Sydney, Australia, April 13, 2012.

▲ Signing the 1,000th autograph of the day, Zayn and the band always take the time to say thanks to those who matter the most—the fans!

ZAYN

Birthplace: Bradford, England

Zodiac sign: Capricorn

Favorite musicians: *NSYNC and Michael Jackson

Favorite color: Black

Hobbies: Drawing

As Zayn captured so perfectly in the *This Is Us* movie—speaking over a funny montage of the band doing some crazy dancing, "We try to stay away from the typical boy band thing, like choreographed dance routines!"

Born in Bradford, England, Zayn's British-Pakistani heritage is something he is very proud of. He also adores his sisters—older sister, Doniya, and two younger sisters, Waliyha and Safaa. Talking to Safaa on the phone when he is thousands of miles away from home is what makes Zayn the happiest. His sisters, of course, follow him on Twitter—along with over 10 million other followers!

▲ Happy and relaxed moments before the Teen Choice Awards, Gibson Amphitheater, Universal City, August 11, 2013.

▲ Fresh-faced Zayn and Liam wave to fans after first appearing on *The X Factor*, December 6, 2010.

▶ Looking so cool... Zayn attends a TV interview in London, England, November 11, 2013.

" I GET TO TRAVEL WITH FOUR OF MY CLOSEST FRIENDS ALL AROUND THE WORLD SO WE KEEP OURSELVES POSITIVE. AND FANS HELP US A LOT AS WELL! "
ZAYN

With his trademark catchphrase of "Vas happening!" (he says it hundreds of times a day, the band reckons!) Zayn also has a collection of nicknames the rest of the band calls him—DJ Malik, Zaynster, and Bradford Bad Boi. And, when it comes to names, Zayn was, of course, born Zain. It was only when he auditioned for *The X Factor* that Zain, sorry, Zayn, changed his name—he thought it looked more interesting.

While all members of the band are now involved in the creative elements of the band's songwriting, it was Zayn who was the first to write part of a song for the band. On their debut single "What Makes You Beautiful" —which went on to sell over five million copies around the world—Zayn wrote the verse that he sings! How amazing is that? Next time you hear the song,

remember that those lyrics are straight from his heart!

As we all know, Zayn is not shy about taking his top off, not because he wants us all to see his body (though we don't mind, do we?) but because he wants to show off his latest tattoos! Now with over 20 (and counting) tattoos, Zayn is the most inked member of One Direction—though Harry is quickly catching up! And Liam, too! How many of Zayn's stunning tattoos can you remember off the top of your head? See if you can count them all. I'll get you started: 1. "Zap!" tattoo on his right arm...

▲ Zayn and his beloved black leather biker jacket at the *This Is Us* film premiere, New York, August 26, 2013.

" LIFE IS FUNNY. THINGS CHANGE, PEOPLE CHANGE, BUT YOU WILL ALWAYS BE YOU, SO STAY TRUE TO YOURSELF AND NEVER SACRIFICE WHO YOU ARE FOR ANYONE."

ZAYN

▲ Walking on their very own red carpet, the 1D boys attend their London, England, premiere of *This Is Us*, August 20, 2013.

▶ One Direction poses for the cameras at the U.S. movie premiere, August 26, 2013.

1D—MOVIE STARS

Filmed in 3D (you no longer have to reach out and touch them anymore, the boys come to you!), the band released their revealing, intimate, and ultra-funny concert movie, *This Is Us,* or as the fans call it, 1D3D, in 2013. The whole world watched!

Directed by acclaimed documentary filmmaker Morgan Spurlock, *This Is Us* has become a box office mega-success in Europe and the U.S.—by far the biggest documentary movie of the year! The movie contains exclusive and never-before-seen footage of the band backstage, nervous and preparing for their shows. Viewers also get an inside look at the gang goofing around with one another, their team, and their families. It is a wonderful 360-degree insight into the band as performers, artists,

▲ At the London premiere of *This Is Us*, Harry gives a little speech in front of Simon Cowell and director Morgan Spurlock, August 20 2013.

◀ "And that's a wrap," Zayn calls the shots, U.S. premiere of 1D3D, August 26, 2013.

teenage boys, best friends, and sons—the scene where Zayn fights back tears after declaring he bought his mom a house is widely considered one of the movie's most beautiful moments.

But it wasn't just the pranks and the fun that the director wanted to capture. Morgan also felt it was his responsibility to express the stress and personal difficulty of what it is like being in the most famous band of the past 20 years. "They have such a great, fun-loving attitude, and you really want to see that shine through, but at the same time they are running a business," the director

" **THERE'S ONLY SO MUCH YOU CAN GET ACROSS ON SOCIAL MEDIA, SO THE MOVIE IS A WAY TO SHOW HOW WE ARE FOR OUR FANS TO SEE.** "
HARRY

explained at the blockbusting New York premiere. "These are five guys who vote on everything that's happening in the band. So I wanted you to see the balance that they deal with, a lot of the stress of their job and this career that they have by goofing off and messing with each other, or security, or the people in their road family. To have that balance is important to them and it was really important for this film."

The film premiered in New York and London in August 2013, and it brought both locations to a standstill. Thousands of screaming fans lined the streets hoping to get a sneak peek of their favorite member of the band, or the group all together.

This Is Us throws an intimate spotlight on what life is like for five best friends in the world's biggest band, and it has very quickly become a sensation all over the world. Released alongside the movie was the brilliantly titled (do we expect anything less?) "Best Song Ever," as melodic and catchy as

everything else the band has released. The song reached high positions in charts all over the world —as did the movie!

Known among fans as "1D3D," the movie takes in Tokyo, New York, and London and is an intimate, engaging, and funny access-all-areas pass into life on the road with our gang of famous singing boys with a spectacular globetrotting day job.

With stunning 3D concert footage of the band's biggest hits woven into behind-the-scenes footage of the boys being boys, clowning and goofing whenever a camera is thrust upon them—the scenes in Japan when Niall and Zayn are wondering what to do with the miso soup are hilarious (and adorable). The film also beautifully captures the meteoric rise of the group from local singers dreaming of the big time to modern pop icons basking in the spotlight of stardom. This is a must-see movie for any Directioner who wants to know what it's like to be a member of One Direction!

▼ Center of attention: the New York premiere of the movie and the band look relaxed before the big unveiling of the film, August 26, 2013.

▲ The night before the very first screening of their film, the band spread the word ... and popcorn... at a conference for the world's press, August 19, 2013.

▲ Harry checks for spelling mistakes at a photo shoot for 1D3D, London, England, August 19, 2013.

▲ The band's very own movie premiere carpet. How cool would it be to have this in your house?

PROFILE:
LIAM

Liam was always going to become a star. After coming so close to solo stardom in the fifth season of *The X Factor* in 2008, it's a good thing Liam was too young that year, otherwise One Direction wouldn't exist today!

Liam may be the band's middleman, but he is a much respected member of the group. While Louis and Zayn are older than him and Niall and Harry are younger, it therefore falls on Liam to be the calming influence in the band, the level-headed one. Liam is the mature member; his big brown eyes and wide smile hint at a more sensible, down-to-earth, and cautious approach to fame and success. The rest of the band credit Liam's sensible attitude with keeping the band together and strong—and they never let him forget it either, with his nickname of Daddy Directioner! Though Liam may disagree with the way the others see him—he considers himself the "clumsy one" in the group after breaking his big toe when he dropped his laptop computer on it in May 2012! The guys haven't let him forget that either!

With his recent clean-cut look—he shaved after Harry made fun of him for copying his trademark floppy locks—and tanned ripped six-pack stomach (a recent development after all the boxing while on the eight month *Take Me Home Tour*), Liam has had the most difficult rise

◀ Look how young he looks! Liam attends the Nickelodeon Kids' Choice Awards, Los Angeles, California, February 21, 2011.

▶ How things change: Liam looking hot in New York, August 26, 2013.

▲ Liam performing at the Vector Center, Auckland, New Zealand, October 12, 2013.

▲ Movie star Liam attending the world premiere of *This Is Us* at the Empire Leicester Square, London, England, August 20, 2013.

◄ The next James Bond? Let's make it happen!

LIAM

Birthplace: Wolverhampton, England

Zodiac sign: Virgo

Favorite musicians: Usher, Justin Timberlake, and Gary Barlow

Favorite color: Purple

Hobbies: Boxing

to fame out of all the band members. In and out of the hospital as a young boy, suffering from a damaged kidney since birth, meant that Liam had to be injected with medicine up to 30 times a day—the poor thing! However, he's all better now.

Liam's first solo auditions on *The X Factor* 2008—when he was just 14 years old—brought a tear of joy to every household in Britain; you could tell he wanted to be a singer so much, he was literally begging Simon and the rest of the judges with such determination on his face! Sadly, it was not to be that year—Mr. Cowell did not believe he was old enough to face the music, and the Live Shows would be too much for a young boy like Liam to manage. In the end, Simon was right. However, Liam is proof that you should never give up on your dreams! After

his first unsuccessful 2008 audition, Liam had the belief, confidence, and determination to try again. This time he finally achieved his goals—worldwide success as a singer, fame, fortune and, of course, his fans!

A brilliant beatboxer, as well as a boxer, Liam describes himself as "not a morning person," which must be tough when the band has to get up early every morning to rehearse, record, and prepare for a live show or public appearance—they don't have many days off either!

The rest of the band members claim that Liam is the most competitive—maybe this is why out of 13 of the 15 tracks on their debut album *Up All Night,* Liam sings the opening verse, beating off the rest of the band, all competing for the lead spot while in the studio!

Along with Zayn and Harry, Liam has a couple of tattoos. The most prominent one

▲ Liam gives his undivided attention to his Directioners, New York, August 23, 2013.

▶ Liam proudly shows off his new buzzcut during Z100's Jingle Ball 2012, Madison Square Garden, New York, December 7, 2012.

—and Liam's favorite—is the line "Everything I Wanted, But Nothing I'll Ever Need," which is scribbled on the back of his right arm. Liam mentions that this is his favorite tattoo, but what does it mean? "It's basically about how obviously we've got a lot of things from being in the band, and there are things that I want in life, but all I ever need is my family and these four boys right here," he said. So sweet!

At school, Liam was the victim of intense bullying, which is one of the main reasons why boxing is so important to him, wanting

to protect himself and those closest to him. "I was bullied by a few people who were much older than me at school, so I went to camp to learn boxing. I was 12, and my coach was 24. I felt like if I could fight him, I could stand up to anyone," Liam said. While bullying at school has greatly affected him, now that he's in One Direction (with four brothers around him) and an expert at boxing, he feels much more secure ... and so do they! While on the American leg of their 2014 *Where We Are Now Tour*, the guys will raise awareness for an anti-bullying campaign that they respect and believe in. And it was Liam's idea to do this! Before each American show, a video will be played to the crowd to help build awareness in schools. "We're really excited to help spread the anti-bullying message with our fans and students in schools across America," explained the band, "And you know we're not long out of school ourselves so we can relate to it. It's a problem that's fresh in our minds and we're eager to raise awareness on this subject." Anti-bullying in schools around the world is important to Liam as

well as the whole band. Support the cause too, if you can.

Liam is also the member of the band who has changed the most visually. He's obviously still figuring out who and what he wants to look like! Liam has had many different hairstyles: long and floppy curls in his early auditions, a brushed-forward style mop-top, an ultra-short army-style buzz cut, and now a slick, short style. What will he do next, we wonder?

Not only has Liam taken up playing the bass—he's getting better, he recently tweeted—he is also a good surfer. While on the Australian leg (the final shows of the year!) of their *Take Me Home Tour*, Liam relished the opportunity to get his hair wet (as well as show off his ripped body to his Australian fans) at the end of 2013, before the guys were due to take some time off. "I really enjoy going on tour in Australia," Liam said in a recent interview. "I'm looking forward to going back, purely for the surfing and the Australian weather." And for the fans too, I'm sure!

BEST. FANS. EVER.

One Direction have the world's greatest fans—and the boys know it. With over 10 million albums sold, and over a billion YouTube video hits, they owe everything to their amazing Directioners.

"**W**e are so thankful to our fans—our success is teamwork between us and them," Louis declared in *This Is Us*, and he is absolutely right. Everywhere they go, every step they take and no matter who they are with, the band's fans are beside them in spirit and in their hearts, making signs up with slogans such as "You're proof that not all heroes wear capes!" and turning up at venues where the band are recording, rehearsing, or performing. And the guys always try to speak and interact with their fans as much as they can. In fact, they relish

▶ Thousands of Directioners line the streets at the movie premiere, Leicester Square, London, England, August 20, 2013.

▼ Niall arrives at the MTV Video Music Awards, Staples Center, Los Angeles, September 6, 2012.

and reciprocate the attention and affection they receive, almost daily, and speak about how amazing their fans are and how special they make them feel.

Known as Directioners, the band's millions of super-fans can enjoy direct contact with their favorite members (or all of them!), thanks to social media sites such as Twitter and Facebook. All of the boys like to reach out and communicate with their fans so if you want to be closer to them, why not follow them all on Twitter! Send them a tweet and see if they tweet you back!

▲ Harry poses for photos while performing live in New York, August 23, 2013.

One Direction's Personal Twitter Feeds

@Harry_Styles
@NiallOfficial
@Louis_Tomlinson
@zaynmalik
@Real_Liam_Payne

At the New York movie premiere of *This Is Us,* at the legendary Rockefeller Plaza, a crowd of 18,000 mega-fans blocked the city's streets, hoping for a glimpse of the band, with many of them lining up five days before the event. This was the largest volume of fans the venue had ever seen and that is saying something!

Since the band's formation, each member has passionately spoken out about how much they adore their fans. Not a day goes by without one of the guys declaring their

" THEY ARE SO DEDICATED ... OUR FANS PUT US WHERE WE ARE."
HARRY

▼ Zayn gives his fans the thumbs up at the U.S. premiere of *This Is Us*, New York.

▲ Hundreds of New York fans stretch to capture Harry's smile.

genuine love—how many other bands do you know that do that?

Sometimes the contact they have with their fans can become over-the-top. One night, after a concert, Liam had managed to get so swamped by Directioners, that he noticed the tour bus he was meant to be on was leaving without him, so he ended up running and screaming after the boys—who all thought he was an over-excited fan!

But that's nothing compared to poor Louis' strangest close-encounter with a Directioner. While in Las Vegas, midway through the U.S. leg of the *Take Me Home*

▲ In honor of National Love Note Day fans leave notes beside the boys' wax figures at Madame Tussauds, New York, September 17, 2013.

Tour, Louis had a visitor at his hotel door: "They knocked on the door of my hotel room," Louis begins, "and I open it in just my boxer shorts, and there was this fan, who just stood there shaking, crying, and I was like 'woah,' what's going on? I closed the door and ran away!" I wonder how often that happens!

Most of the time, however, the guys are extremely happy to pose for photos, play around, and joke with their fans, especially those Directioners who have traveled great distances to see them perform or who have gone to the effort of creating some amazing fan-art or signs that declare how much they love the band!

" FEEL FREE TO INSULT ME, BUT YOU DON'T HAVE THE RIGHT TO INSULT OUR FANS."
LOUIS

▲ 1D meeting Japanese fans to promote *This Is Us*, Chiba, Japan, November 3, 2013.

▶ Playing the Makuhari Messe Arena, the boys fly high and wow the Japanese crowd, November 2, 2013.

1D IN AUSTRALIA AND JAPAN

The boys' grueling work schedules and tours fling them all over the world, from London to Tokyo, Melbourne to Auckland, and *everywhere* in between.

One Direction loves nothing more than to see the world, which is convenient considering in summer 2013, the MTV VMAs gave the band the Best Worldwide Act gong! Liam, super-excited by the prospect of a "world tour" since his earliest *X Factor* auditions, had that dream realized when they embarked on a 130-date arena tour around the globe in winter of 2013. The tour included a 26-date jaunt across Australia and New Zealand—playing to a staggering 81,000 fans across their seven Sydney shows alone.

Will One Direction do the Fresh Prince of Bel Air Rap for us?

Roulaa Konstandis

Section 5, Row R, Seat 61

While completing this section of the *Take Me Home Tour,* some of the guys were seen getting sun- and sea-soaked while surfing and unwinding from the previous nights' chaotic shows in Melbourne, where Harry started to eat noodles on stage and and wave a carrot around.

While at a gig in Sydney—the band's first show on the final leg of the *Take Me Home Tour,* the band replied to a tweet sent to them live onstage by a member of the audience. The tweet was "Will One Direction do the Fresh Prince rap for us?" They did it brilliantly—with Liam providing the beat and each member singing a part. Check out the video of them doing it on YouTube!

During the song "Kiss You" as well a for a few other ballads mid-set, the bar performed on a platform that suspende them high above and out toward the crow As if singing live wasn't scary enough!

During one of the opening shows of th *Take Me Home Tour* in Adelaide, just aft the band had been play fighting with wat pistols, Louis slipped onstage and fell in fro of tens of thousands of fans, much to h embarrassment. Not to worry, the rest of th band rushed over to see if he was OK, helpe picked him up, and then carried on li nothing had happened—true professionals

The band first went to Japan early in 20 and their visit can be seen in the *This Is L* movie—with the band filmed wearing (ar

▲ Reaching the end of the *Take Me Home Tour*, the exhausted band take a break and promote 1D3D, Chiba, Japan, November 3, 2013.

◀ The 1D boys Fresh Prince rap at the Hordern Pavilion, Sydney, Australia, April 13, 2012.

fooling around in, of course) traditional Japanese dress, known as Kimonos. The hysteria that greeted and followed the band for the brief time they were there was incredible. While only in Japan for a few public appearances, they were super excited! Niall tweeted, "Japan! This place is so cool! Can't wait for the next few days! Gonna be fun! Airport was crazy! Big love to Japanese fans."

Toward the final leg of the *Take Me Home Tour,* the boys stopped to play a couple of mega-massive shows at Toyko's Makuhari Masse venue and performed in front of more than 20,000 fans.

▲ 20,000 fans show their support with homemade signs and mass sing-a-longs, Hisense Arena, Melbourne, Australia, October 24, 2013.

PROFILE:
HARRY

Harry Styles—if there is a cooler name in pop music right now then we have yet to meet him. And we don't want to—because Harry is all we need!

Perhaps the most visible member of the band due to his trademark flop of curly hair, his beautiful movie-star good looks, and his high-profile relationships with famous TV presenters and singers, Harry also caused quite a stir with his controversial tattoos —the first one creating a global interest. He now has over 20!

Born on February 1, 1994 to Anne and Des Styles in the sleepy town of Homes Chapel, Cheshire, England, heartthrob Harry (as the fans nicknamed him) has an older sister named Gemma, who he often talks about and who can often be seen at his gigs—she clearly adores her little brother.

Harry wears his fame with style (!), goofiness, and a level head. It's obvious that he has a long and amazing career ahead of him, no matter what he does! As Rihanna said, "he has star quality," that X Factor, the magic ingredient that has made all the band's fans fall in love with him. He also has that massive, gorgeous smile that can be seen from outer space. The whole world adores him and he has a legion of female fans of all ages. Whoever finally marries him will be one lucky lady, but we don't expect wedding bells just yet. Harry has been linked to a number of famous girls over the past three years including country singer Taylor Swift, and even Oscar-winner Jennifer Lawrence.

◀ Bearly-famous: A young Harry spotted arriving at Fountain Studios, London, England, December 3, 2010.

▲ Harry taking care of business on *The X Factor U.K.* tour, Wembley Arena, London, England, March 6, 2011.

▲ En route to the show: Harry waves to his rain-soaked admirers, Auckland, New Zealand, October 12, 2013.

HARRY

Birthplace: Doncaster, England

Zodiac sign: Aquarius

Favorite musicians: The Beatles, Elvis Presley, and Coldplay

Favorite colors: Orange and blue

Hobbies: Tennis and badminton

Harry was only 16 when he first auditioned for the *The X Factor* in 2010, and he is one of the youngest contestants that the show has ever put through to its final stages. The judges all noted his maturity beyond his years, and could all tell from the audience's reaction that he was going to be the next big thing. They were right; Harry just needed a push in the right direction.

Before his big break on *The X Factor*, Harry was working part-time at a bakery in his hometown of Cheshire, as seen wonderfully in *This Is Us*, when Harry returns home and visits his former colleagues.

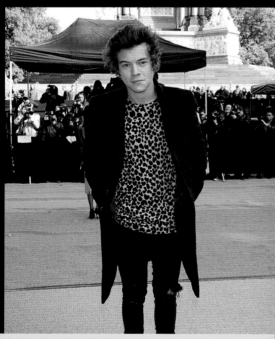

▲ Looking fine: Harry arrives at the Burberry 2014 show during London Fashion Week, September 16, 2013.

▲ Harry shares a joke with Kelly Osbourne, London Fashion Week, September 14, 2013.

▶ Model of the year? Harry looking cool in a plaid shirt, New York, August 23, 2013.

▼ Harry clearly has something to smile about in September 2013. What's caught his eye, we wonder?

▲ Harry gives the fans directions at the Nationwide Arena, Columbus, Ohio, July 18, 2013.

Pre-fame, Harry wasn't just a baker's assistant. He also performed with his indie band White Eskimo—check out the video of them playing "Summer of 69" at a friend's wedding on YouTube just before Harry auditioned for *The X Factor*. They're really talented ... but not as good as 1D, obviously.

Goofy, intelligent, brooding, intense, and with a great sense of humor and quick wit—not to mention a keen eye for sharp clothes and fashion—Harry has it all. On their debut record, it is Harry's voice we hear the most, with over seven minutes of solo time. His body (along with Zayn's) is also the one we see the most. "Stripping off is very liberating, I feel so free!" he once exclaimed.

Despite being regularly labeled as one of the hunkiest men in the world, Harry takes all the fame, attention, and adoration with maturity way beyond his years.

And it's not just the rest of the world that has fallen in love with Harry – his bandmates have too! As the youngest member of the band, the rest of group look upon Harry as their little brother, fiercely protective and loyal. But because Harry is the most high-profile member of the band, the other guys all look up to him too, and they respect how well adjusted he has become to stardom. If only all young male singers were like Harry!

▲ Harry shows off his movie star style in his favorite look (button down shirts!), New York, August 26, 2013.

▼ Taking a dip: Harry shows off his tattoos while on a well-deserved day off in Miami, Florida, June 16, 2013.

" WHEN I WAS LITTLE I KNEW I WANTED TO ENTERTAIN PEOPLE."
HARRY

▲ Liam gets a touch of makeup before a New York performance, August 2013.

▶ Lady Gaga and the boys hang out together at the 2013 MTV Video Music Awards, New York.

1D BOYS WILL BE BOYS

If there is one thing One Direction are more famous for than their infectious pop songs, it's their behind-the-scenes videos and pranks they play on each other while off-duty!

All five members of the band are renowned funsters—even "sensible" Liam!—always trying their best to outdo each other with pranks and stunts and, basically, making as much fun of each other as possible and making each other laugh during serious TV and radio interviews when live on air.

The band's scores of YouTube, Vine, and Twitter videos and pictures are also extremely funny—not to mention crazy!—and they always show off the band in high spirits.

Over the years, the pranks that they pull on each other have become more and more

▲ Getting cozy before the show: The band takes a break before going crazy at the Patriot Center, Fairfax, Vancouver, March 2, 2012.

◄ Valentine's Day gig: On the day of the release of "What Makes You Beautiful," the band performed for their French fans, Paris, February 14, 2013.

elaborate—whether they are driving around in golf carts backstage or dressing up in fancy clothes! One of the most notorious pranks the band played on each other was when Louis and Zayn hired an actress to portray a pregnant TV producer and pretend she was going into labor while backstage at a Nickelodeon recording. The whole prank is caught on camera and Harry's intense face, in reaction to the stunt, is priceless.

Have you ever seen the boys standing still and not talking? It's very rare—usually they are all too busy running around having fun! But on one occasion, during some

" I WOULDN'T SAY I'M GIRL-CRAZY, BUT I AM QUITE FLIRTY. MAYBE TOO FLIRTY."
HARRY

> ## " WE'RE NOT PERFECT. WE'RE TRYING TO BE OURSELVES."
> LOUIS

well-deserved downtime from recording the *Midnight Memories* album, the boys headed to London's Madame Tussauds and pretended to pose as wax figures for the afternoon! Of course, they couldn't keep still for long and soon started to surprise and shock the fans who came up to them to pose for photos—much to their (and the fans') delight! "Oh, my, god, I swear I just saw Liam move!" one fan screamed!

But perhaps one of the funniest, and most embarrassing, pranks the band have played on each other was when waiting for food at a Burger King at a gas station when Louis pulled down Niall's pants—in front of some unsuspecting fans who were filming the hungry boys. This rare moment of the boys being out-and-about—and not swamped by fans—shows the band at their most honest, just being themselves and having fun with each other like boys do. They are friends first, bandmates second and that is a rare thing in the music industry. The video was an online hit with over 500,000 YouTube views so far! "I had nice Calvin Klein's on," remembers Niall, "but I was so embarrassed."

◀ Get out of the way: Harry arrives at his Belgium hotel surrounded by fans, press, and security, May 2013.

▲ Take that: Niall gets back at pesky paparazzi photographers!

▶ Zayn gets his leg tattooed, Weymouth, England, May 15, 2013.

PROFILE:
LOUIS

The band's oldest member, Louis, also goes by many other nicknames given to him by the band—Tommo, Lou, and Boobear! Not only just one fifth of One Direction, Louis is a pretty amazing piano player, soccer player, and heartthrob, too...

Born Louis Troy Austin, Louis may be the oldest of the group (by over a year), but he is definitely the most immature, stating once that he'd like to remain "immature forever" —young at heart, that's Louis!

With his obsession for wearing striped T-shirts and sweatshirts (he must have a wardrobe full of them), not to mention sleepwalking (the rest of the band have all caught him at various times), the messiest member of One Direction also once got expelled from school after he flashed his butt to his principal, making him the boldest member of the band, too!

Louis famously met his fellow bandmate (and roommate, they share a house together) Harry in the bathroom backstage during an audition for *The X Factor*, and the two formed one of the strongest bonds in modern pop history—being the oldest and youngest members of the band, they possibly formed a bond through their well-

◀ Spex factor: Louis arriving at the Brighton Center, England, on *The X Factor* tour, March 16, 2011.

▶ Model man: Louis attends the Teen Choice Awards, Gibson Amphitheater, California, August 11, 2013.

▲ Louis thanks the fans onstage at the Teen Choice Awards, Gibson Amphitheater, California, August 11, 2013

▲ Louis the movie star: Attending his own red carpet premiere, London, England, August 2013.

◀ Making waves on his day off: Louis looks bronzed on Australia's Gold Coast, October 2013.

LOUIS

Birthplace: Doncaster, England

Zodiac sign: Capricorn

Favorite musicians: The Fray and Robbie Williams

Favorite color: Red

Hobbies: Soccer

documented acts of immaturity and silliness, as well as being the two members of the group who are often voted the "hottest," regularly appearing in the "World's Sexiest Men Alive" polls! Although, Zayn isn't far behind either—or Liam—or Niall!

With six tattoos—a moose and a heart, a piece of rope, a pointy finger, a bird, The Rogue (written on his legs), and "It is what it is" scribbled across his chest, Louis doesn't quite have as many tattoos as Harry and Zayn, but he's catching up. While on tour in New Zealand in October 2013, both Zayn and Louis got new tattoos—Louis got a Pac-Man on his arm and a spider's web on his leg!

Born on Christmas Eve in 1991, Louis was a busy boy when he auditioned for *The X Factor* in 2010—he was working part-time at the local cinema and as a waiter, studying at

▲ Premiere poser: Louis makes his fans' day by posing for a photograph, London, England, August 20, 2013.

▶ Playing up: Louis before a charity soccer game at Celtic Park, Glasgow, Scotland, September 8, 2013.

high school and attending acting school in his spare time. He's a hard worker, for sure!

Though the whole band are all fans of the game, and can often be seen kicking a ball around backstage and for local charity matches, Louis is without doubt the most soccer-obsessed member of the band, having once been signed semi-professionally as a youngster for his local soccer team, the Doncaster Rovers. So talented!

AT SCHOOL I WAS ALWAYS THAT GUY THAT WAS MAKING PEOPLE LAUGH."
LOUIS

▲ During rehearsals in Sydney, Australia, Louis likes to keep his legs busy, October 2013.

◀ Louis relaxing backstage at the V Festival, England, August 2013.

▲ LOL—Louis Out Loud: the 1D superstar being interviewed in New York, August 23, 2013.

"WE LIKE TO THINK WE'RE ROCK 'N' ROLL BUT WE'RE NOT REALLY."
LOUIS

▲ Close to their fans: Onstage during the MTV Video Music Awards, Staples Center, Los Angeles, September 2012.

▶ Celebrating in style: Winning the Global Success Award at the BRIT Awards ceremony, London, February 2013.

1D—WINNERS!

In their first three years, One Direction have not only sold millions of records, they have also won scores of trophies, gongs, and Moonmen from some of the biggest award ceremonies in the world.

But if all the awards and world domination wasn't enough (and it clearly isn't!), the band has also broken numerous world records, too! Not only are they the youngest artists ever to have a simultaneous number one album and single, they are also one of a very small handful of artists in the history of recorded music to have released two number one albums within the same year!

In 2012, the *Guinness Book of World Records* awarded the band the rarest achievement in the music industry—to be the first British group (EVER!) in U.S. chart history

▲ 1D won Song of the Summer for "Best Song Ever" at the MTV Video Music Awards at the Barclays Center, New York, August 2013.

◀ 1D are interviewed at the MTV Video Music Awards, New York, August 2013.

to have a debut album go to number one in the U.S. Billboard charts. "Being the first British band to debut at Number 1 in America with a debut album is something that we would never even have dreamt of. We are incredibly proud to have this achievement included in the *Guinness World Records* book," the band said after learning of their phenomenal achievement.

But the world record-breaking doesn't stop there. The *Guinness Book of World Records* also gave the band the coveted award for "Highest debut by a U.K. group on the U.S. singles chart" with the song

"BEING THE FIRST BRITISH BAND TO DEBUT AT NUMBER 1 IN AMERICA WITH A DEBUT ALBUM IS SOMETHING THAT WE WOULD NEVER EVEN HAVE DREAMT OF."
ONE DIRECTION

"Live While We're Young." *And even that is not enough...*

In 2013, it also became official that One Direction were the "Most followed pop group on Twitter," as officiated by the *Guinness World Records* again. That's quite an achievement for five teenage boys from England and Ireland! It's doubtful that these records will ever be beaten.

In the summer of 2013 though, the band, well, Harry, won the most prestigious award on the planet—"Best Look," at

Justin Timberlake, Lady Gaga, and Rihanna

However, as the guys themselves would agree, none of their fame and fortune is comparable to the love and support they receive from their fans from all over the world. It is thanks to each and every loyal fan that every member of One Direction is now more famous than you (or they!) could eve have dreamt of! With the release of *Midnigh Memories*, nobody can predict what awards they will win next or where they'll be in ter years' time. But one thing is for certain—it's

◀ The band accepts the Best Pop Video award at the MTV Video Music Awards, Staples Center, Los Angeles, September 6, 2012.

▲ Fresh from performing "Live While We're Young," the band collects a Bambi Award, Düsseldorf, Germany, November 22, 2012.

▲ The boys arrive at the Teen Choice Awards, Gibson Amphitheater, Universal City, California, August 11, 2013.

▲ The band wins Choice Group Award at the Teen Choice Awards, Gibson Amphitheater, Universal City, California, August 11, 2013.

PICTURE CREDITS

The publishers would like to thank the following sources for their kind permission to reproduce the pictures in this book.

Key, t=top, l=left, r=right, c=center, b=bottom

Corbis: R.Chiang/Splash News (8), Grant Hodgson/Splash News (67b), JC/Splash News (14), London Ent/Splash News (11tr), Grey Wasp/Splash News (57), James Whatling/Splash News (28-29, 30), Splash News (9, 61t, 64-65, 75b, 81l, 85l, 89l)

Getty Images: Gianni Barbieux/Photonews (80), Dave M. Benett (49br, 72c, 85r), Larry Busacca (44-45), Gilbert Carrasquillo/FilmMagic (4-5), David Fisher (49t), Fox (42), Ian Gavan (47, 53r, 86), Steve Granitz (83), Marc Grimwade/WireImage (16), Ian Horrocks/Newcastle United (18, 26t), Brian Killian (55), Dan Kitwood (58-59), Jon Kopaloff/FilmMagic (95bl), Peter Kramer/NBC/NBC NewsWire (20, 73), Jason LaVeris/FilmMagic (19), Kevin Mazur/WireImage (12t, 17l, 40b, 49bl, 60, 76-77, 92), Kevin Mazur/Fox/WireImage (84), Neil Mockford/FilmMagic (68), NBC NewsWire (54), Cindy Ord/Madame Tussauds (62), Ryan Pierse (38), Rich Polk/WireImage (25, 27b, 56, 58, 90), Ben Stansall/AFP (90-91), Mark Sullivan/WireImage (27t), Keith Tsuji (64, 67t), Tim P. Whitby (17r), Stuart C. Wilson (72b), Kevin

Photoshot: Imago (39), LFI (37), Picture Alliance (43) Furniss, Invision (44), Doug Peters/Empics Entertainment (41, 46) Charles Sykes/AP (62-63), Dennis Van Tine/ABACA USA/Empics Entertainment (89r), Ian West/PA Wire (53l, 96)

Rex Features: Akem Photos (21l), Matt Baron (36, 79), Beretta, Sims (82), Broadimage (11br, 69), Toure Cheick (78), Fred Cornish/Bournemouth News (81r), Jonathan Hordle (72t), IBL (34, 35), Henry Lamb/Photowire/BEI (1), James McCauley (22-23), McCormack/Knotek (88), Ross McDairmant Photography (87), McPix Ltd (40t), MediaPunch (6-7), Most Wanted (95t) Newspix (22l), Erik Pendzich (12, 76), PictureGroup (26b), Picture Perfect (93), Brian Rasic (70), David Rowland (24, 52), Simon Runting (71), Willi Schneider (33), Startraks Photo (3, 15, 48, 51 61b), Graham Stone (50), Nikki To (66), Zuma (10-11, 74-75)

Every effort has been made to acknowledge correctly and contact the source and/or copyright holder of each picture and the publisher apologizes for any unintentional errors which will be corrected in future editions o